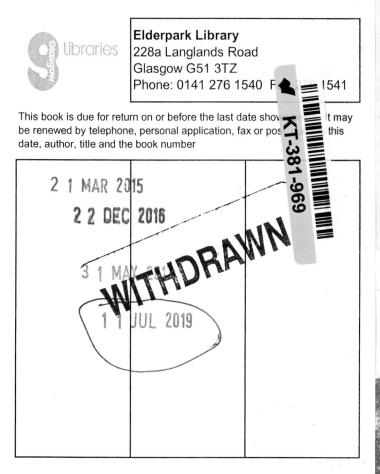

First published 2014 by Walker Entertainment,
an imprint of Walker Books Ltd, 87 Vauxhall Walk, London SE11 5HJ

4 6 8 10 9 7 5 3

Written by Martin Howard and illustrated by Andy Janes
© and TM Aardman Animations Limited 2014

This book has been typeset in Manticore

Printed and bound in Great Britain by Clays Ltd, St Ives plc

British Library Cataloguing in Publication Data:
a catalogue record for this book is available from the British Library

ISBN 978-1-4063-5772-1

www.walker.co.uk

Tales from Mossy Bottom Farm

THE **BEAST** OF SOGGY MOOR

Martin Howard

illustrated by Andy Janes

WALKER
ENTERTAINMENT

SHAUN is the leader of the Flock. He's clever, cool and always keeps his head when the other sheep are losing theirs.

BITZER

The Farmer's faithful dog and a good friend to Shaun, Bitzer's the ever suffering sheepdog, doing his best to keep Shaun's pals out of trouble.

THE FARMER

Running the farm with Bitzer at his side, the Farmer is completely oblivious to the human-like intelligence of his flock ... or their stupidity.

THE FLOCK

One big happy (if slightly dopey) family, the sheep like to play and create mischief together, though it's usually Shaun and Bitzer who sort out the resulting mess.

NUTS

Nuts is the zaniest sheep around. His crazy exploits are always getting him into trouble. Luckily Shaun is on hand to help him out.

THE BEAST

Aaaarroo! The beast is on the prowl, and it's hungry...

CONTENTS

CHAPTER ONE

THE SILENCE OF THE SHEEP

Mist oozed through the meadow, creeping into the farmyard from Soggy Moor. Deep, sleepy snores shook the rafters of the Mossy Bottom Farm barn. Lit by moonbeams shining through cracks in the walls, the Flock slept, their snores broken by a horrible slurping, lip-smacking sound. In her dream, Shirley was doing breaststroke through a sea of cake.

But not everyone on Mossy Bottom Farm was sleeping. Bats twittered around the crumbling chimneys of the farmhouse. A single light burned in a high window. Silhouetted, the Farmer trimmed his nose hair with a pair of garden shears.

And below, someone or something padded through the farmyard on silent paws – a dark figure with mist curling around its ankles. It was making a low growling noise that got louder with every step. Hunger gnawing at its stomach, it peered around in the moonlight.

A tiny bit of drool leaked from the corner of its mouth.

It was starving.

It needed to feed.

Bones, it thought to itself. Lovely fresh bones. And a cup of tea.

Bitzer stepped out of the fog and stopped by a gate where a crooked sign was hung.

His stomach grumbled again. Embarrassed, Bitzer patted it, wishing he'd brought a biscuit with him. Evening rounds were almost finished, though. Soon, he could settle down for a quiet night in with his favourite bone and a cup of tea. Now, what was left to do?

He checked his clipboard. The Flock were tucked up in the barn, the Farmer was in the farmhouse, the ducks were playing a late-night game of cards and the pigs were snoring like bulldozers. But there was something he had forgotten. Muttering to himself, he flipped a page and peered at it in the moonlight. The chickens! After jabbing the clipboard with his pencil, he set off towards the hen house, humming, "Pum pum pa puuum."

The bush rustled. Bitzer's ears twitched. Just the wind, he told himself as he arrived at the chicken coop and went inside.

One chicken, two chickens, three chickens... Bitzer ticked them off his list, grinning to himself, when Beryl clucked in dozy surprise and laid an egg in her sleep. Breakfast had arrived.

Four chickens, five chickens— AAAA

Bitzer's knees started to knock. He couldn't go outside; there was something out there. Something that didn't sound at all friendly. In fact, it sounded like it gobbled sheepdogs for breakfast.

Bitzer clutched his paws together pleadingly. He was too young to be gobbled up. Could he stay a little longer? He'd be very, very quiet. The chickens wouldn't know he was there. Wouldn't the chickens feel safer with a dog to protect them?

The cockerel sniffed, fixed him with a beady eye and pointed with his wing again. OUT!

Bitzer peered outside. The moon shone down. Nothing moved but the bats and the silhouette of the Farmer, which was hopping up and down, clutching its nose. Bitzer gulped.

He wasn't afraid, he told himself with a nervous chuckle. Oh no, it would take more than a silly howl to scare him. He was the kind of dog that licked the face of fear. Besides, the howling was probably just Shaun up to his usual tricks.

Bitzer nodded. *Yes, that was it.* Shaun would be out there, a sheet over his head, ready to jump out and scare him. Well, Bitzer did not scare easily. After tucking the clipboard under his arm, he marched out of the hen house.

AAAAAARRRROOOOOOooooooooooo!

Bitzer threw his clipboard into the air with a yelp. Shaun hadn't made that terrifying sound. And if Shaun hadn't ... what had?

Clouds rolled away from the moon. Long shadows fell across the dark meadow. There, outlined against the wall of the barn, was the shadow of a ...

... BEAST!

CHAPTER TWO

THINGS THAT GO "AAAARRROO!" IN THE NIGHT

The barn shook as the door slammed with a CRASH! Shaun's eyes flashed opened to see Bitzer spreadeagled against it. He looked terrified. One by one, the Flock opened their eyes and stretched. They stared at the petrified Bitzer. Shirley pushed her sleep mask up. After peeling the slices of cucumber from her eyes, she popped them into her mouth. Meanwhile, Nuts, thinking it was morning, began his daily exercise routine with a few push-ups and sheep dips. With a yawn, Timmy poked his mum: *Breakfast time.*

A face dripping green slime lifted its head.

"Waaaaah!" Bitzer goggled at it, gargling with fear.

Blinking, Shaun looked from Bitzer to Timmy's Mum. It was true she didn't look at her best covered in Wrinkle-B-Gone, age-defying night-cream, but she wasn't *that* scary. Shaun threw off his blanket and then prodded Bitzer. What was wrong with him?

A fresh shiver ran down Bitzer's spine as he remembered the terrible shadow against the barn wall. With an effort, he forced his knees to stop knocking. He had to warn

the Flock about ... the beast! He pulled his face into a nasty, drooling snarl.

Shaun frowned. Was it toothache?

Bitzer shook his head and tried again. This time, his eyes rolled wildly and he gnashed his teeth. It was horrible. *Horrible!*

Shaun nodded. He thought he understood what had happened. Had Bitzer heard the Farmer practising his trombone again? He patted the sheepdog sympathetically. It was enough to upset anyone.

By now, Bitzer was jumping with frustration. He stretched out his claws and growled, pointing at the door. A savage beast was prowling Mossy Bottom Farm.

Shaun chuckled. A savage beast? The only savage beast on Mossy Bottom Farm was in Bitzer's imagination, although – he had to admit – one or two of the ducks could get quite nasty if their breakfast didn't arrive on time.

Bitzer made the beast face again, this time with extra snarling. The beast was out there. He had seen it! It was huge, with enormous jaws and teeth like hedge trimmers.

Shaun patted Bitzer again. It had been bound to happen. The stress of standing by the gate all day watching sheep had been too much. Bitzer's mind had snapped. He had gone completely bonkers.

Shaun bleated kindly. He would take Bitzer back to his kennel. Bitzer would feel better after a good night's sleep.

A curl of mist oozed into the barn as Shaun pulled the door open. With a whimper, Bitzer slammed it shut again.

A sudden, fearful bleat made Shaun look round. Hazel was shivering beneath a sack, with a terrified look in her eyes. She shook her head slowly. Bitzer wasn't mad. There was a beast. She had heard the stories from her mum when she was just a tiny lamb.

A monster prowled the moor beyond Mossy Bottom Farm. Once, Hazel had heard its ghastly wail in the dead of night. "Aaarooooo-owwww!" she bleated in a low whisper.

Bitzer nodded in excitement. Yes. *Yes!* The beast had sounded exactly like that! He glared at Shaun. Now did he believe?

Shaun rolled his eyes. He heard strange noises in the night all the time. Usually they were made by Shirley.

Timmy's Mum bleated nervously. She remembered being awoken one dark night – a night just like this one – by the sound of some hideous creature devouring its prey. It had made a ghastly, slurping, chewing noise.

Shaun sighed, shaking his head. Shirley yet again, he thought to himself. There was nothing to be frightened of—

Scraaattch.

The barn was filled with bleats of terror.
Sheep dived under their blankets.

Quivering like jellies, everyone stared
at the door. There was *something* outside.
Something that was trying to get in! The
beast had come to eat them!

Timmy sucked his dummy and giggled happily. He loved hide-and-seek. After putting his hands over his eyes, he began counting to ten, bleating with disappointment when his mum scooped him up and set him down behind her. Growling, she picked up the first weapon she could lay a hoof on. If the beast came for Timmy it would get ... she glanced down ... a fight with a carrot it would never forget.

Shirley whimpered. She was so plump and juicy the beast was bound to come for her first. But perhaps it might leave her alone if there were two sheep to eat instead. Hoping no one was looking, she edged behind the Twins.

Scraaattch.

Shaun blinked at the door. He had been sure Bitzer was making the beast up, but there was definitely something outside. Maybe it was just the branches of a tree blowing against the door ... except there weren't any trees near the barn. He gulped, then took a deep breath.

And, with his heart in his mouth, Shaun opened the door.

Bitzer nodded at him. *Go on.* Then he covered his eyes, peering between his paws and whining as Shaun stepped out into the night.

Shaun shrugged and bleated. There was nothing outside but a swirl of mist.

Bitzer dropped his paws. He took a sniff, then a small step outside. Shaun crossed his arms and tapped a hoof. Bitzer noticed that sheep were staring at him. Embarrassed, he gave a small cough, then trotted out to stand by Shaun. He looked about and barked.

The beast had gone. He – Bitzer – must've frightened it away.

Shaun sighed as the Flock burst into applause. Bitzer puffed out his chest. The Flock had nothing to be afraid of while Bitzer was there to protect them.

Shaun growled softly in Bitzer's ear.

The sheepdog yelped, jumping three foot in the air.

Heh, heh, heh, Shaun snickered behind his hoof.

CHAPTER THREE

WHO'S AFRAID OF THE BIG, BAD BEAST?

Bitzer squeezed his eyes closed and turned over, mumbling for just another five minutes' sleep. Shaun prodded him again. Bitzer was harder to wake up than a box of hedgehogs. He looked around, grinning to himself as his eyes settled on a bucket of water.

Spluttering and spitting, Bitzer sat up. As Hazel threw the barn doors open, memories of the night before came flooding back. With a shiver, Bitzer pulled his sack blanket up to his nose, eyes darting about nervously. The beast? Had it gone?

Outside, birds twittered and a cockerel crowed an only slightly grumpy alarm call. The fog had vanished. In the distance, Shaun could see the Farmer. He had a bandaged nose and was clanking empty slop buckets by the pigsty. As he bent to refill them, he clonked his head on the corner of the trough. "Waaaarrgh ... oooooowww!" he wailed.

Shaun chuckled to himself. The Farmer was always clumsy. The week before he had managed to run over his own thumb with the wheelbarrow. People all the way down in Mossy Bottom village had heard him wailing.

Shaun nudged Bitzer again and tapped a hoof impatiently. It was time for breakfast. Was he going to do his morning rounds, or was he too scared?

Shaun tried not to smile as Bitzer gave him a chilly look and wrung water out of his hat. The only reason Bitzer had stayed in the barn all night was to guard the Flock. It would take more than a silly beast to scare Bitzer the guard dog.

Ignoring Shaun's grin, he settled his hat on his head, strolled out into the meadow and picked up his muddy clipboard. He didn't have time to stand around chatting all day.

As Shaun watched Bitzer head into the hen house, he hatched a plan for later. He sniggered, imagining Bitzer's reaction when—

Bitzer flew out of the hen house, yowling in panic, followed by an explosion of feathers and terrified chickens.

The beast! The BEAST!

THE BEAST HAD STRUCK!

Bitzer stood panting in the middle of a ring of sheep, jabbing at his clipboard with a trembling paw. One of chickens was missing. The beast had taken her! Mossy Bottom Farm was in the clutches of a rampaging monster.

They were all DOOMED!

Bitzer howled again.

But ... but ... surely the beast only existed in Bitzer's imagination? It wasn't real! Shaun swallowed. It couldn't be true. There must be some mistake.

Nuts interrupted with a low bleat. There was no mistake. He, too, had heard stories of the beast. His dear old grandpa had told him it was a terrible creature. It was huge and covered in black and white hair, with horns, and its howl was a dreadful "Moo!" that made a sheep's blood run cold.

Bitzer shook his head. Nuts' beast sounded nasty, but this one was worse. He pointed at the tractor. The shadow of the beast had been that big. And it had teeth as long as ... as... He pointed at an old pickaxe leaning against the barn, and it had three ... no, five ... heads.

An ever increasing circle of faces gawped at him. Terror had spread across Mossy Bottom Farm like wildfire. Every frightened animal wanted to know more about the beast. Chickens huddled together, clucking nervously. How many hens could the beast eat?

All of them, thought Bitzer to himself.

The other animals read the thought from the look of horror on his face. With a cluck, Beryl fell back in a dead faint, her legs in the air.

"Squeee!" One of the pigs leaned over the wall. When he was a piglet, his dad had told him of a big, bad creature who huffed and puffed and blew little pigs up.

The other pigs frowned. No, that was wrong. The beast dragged pigs off to market ... or something like that. Roast beef and wee wee were involved. It was horrible.

Hazel cleared her throat. She rubbed her tummy. The beast was always hungry, or so she had heard.

Shirley shook herself, fluffing up her wool until she was double the size. The beast was huge. A friend of a friend had said so.

The Twins pulled their lips back, glaring and drooling. The beast was ferocious. Only the worst kind of monster would eat a chicken.

Shaun jumped onto an upturned barrel, bleating for everyone to stop. None of the animals were going to be eaten. Bitzer wouldn't allow it ... would he?

The animals looked around.

Bitzer was nowhere to be seen.

Beryl came round from her swoon, screamed a clucky scream, and fainted again. The beast had taken Bitzer!

A terrified babbling broke out. Bitzer had been snatched away! The beast was among them. And it was *invisible*!

With a bleat, Shaun pointed. It was all right. Bitzer was over by the doghouse, and he was making some home improvements.

The animals of Mossy Bottom Farm peered questioningly through the ring of barbed wire, with a small sentry post, that Bitzer had put up. The sheepdog, wearing an upside-down colander on his head, was barricading his kennel.

Bitzer, ashamed, shuffled his feet. He wasn't afraid – oh no, no, no, no, no. He was just taking a few precautions.

With a shake of his head, Shaun gestured at the moors that surrounded Mossy Bottom Farm. They couldn't barricade the whole farm. Someone had to hunt the beast.

Bitzer gulped. "Wh-wh-wh-whuff," he agreed, trembling.

Timmy's Mum clasped her hooves together. Bitzer was a hero.

Shaun stared at the sky and whistled quietly while counting in his head: One, two, three...

Bitzer blinked around at the circle of animals and made the shape of a beast with his paws. It was quite a large beast, wasn't it?

Four, counted Shaun.

Bitzer barked again. Because it was such a massive creature, he would need help. He turned to Shaun with a sickly sweet, pleading smile.

Five.

Shaun rolled his eyes. It had taken Bitzer just five seconds to rope him in.

CHAPTER FOUR

THE TRAIL TO SOGGY MOOR

As mist crept across the farmyard and a full
moon rose in the sky, Shaun tied a strip of
old sack around his head. Then, while taking
a deep breath, he opened the barn door and
crept out, keeping low to the ground.

There was a light in the bathroom window
of the farmhouse and the distant sound of
running water. Shaun grinned to himself,
wondering if the Farmer would get the

43

temperature of the bath water right tonight. Last time, it had been scalding hot, and the Farmer's foot had looked like a ripe tomato for the next three days.

SIZZLE

Shaun peered into the gloom. All his sheep senses were alert, and his heart was drumming in his chest. The moonlight cast strange shadows. Shaun caught his breath, crouching lower as he spotted the shape of a ghastly creature with a flying-saucer-shaped head lurching towards him through the fog. Shaun's heart skipped a beat before he realized it was only Bitzer, in his colander helmet.

Bitzer heard a chuckle and blinked nervously. The beast was close, and it was laughing at him! He yelped when Shaun touched him on the shoulder.

Shaun bleated. If they were going to track the beast, Bitzer had to stop being so jumpy.

Bitzer grinned to cover his embarrassment. He wasn't scared. He'd known it was Shaun all along. He'd just been joking around.

It was time to go on a beast hunt...

47

Bitzer rolled his eyes. The pants belonged to the Farmer. They must have blown off the washing line. Sheep were rubbish at tracking, but dogs were brilliant hunters. His nose was already twitching. Bitzer stiffened, catching a scent. His eyes lit up. He was on the trail! Sniffing at the ground, tail wagging, he disappeared into the fog, zigzagging across the moor as his powerful nose led him onwards.

Shaun blinked in surprise, then followed. He hadn't expected Bitzer to be so fearless, but the sheepdog was running ahead, snuffling and whuffing with excitement as the trail got stronger. There was yelp, then a growling, slobbering sound.

Bitzer had found something!

Puffing with effort, Shaun raced through the mist until he caught up. He emerged from the fog to find that Bitzer had wrestled his prey to the floor and was shaking it roughly, drops of slobber flying through the air as he sank his teeth into it.

Shaun bleated. What had Bitzer found? Was it the beast?

Bitzer looked up happily. Between his teeth was a large bone. His eyes darted left and right. Was the beast near by? It couldn't have his bone. He would defend it with his life.

Shaun tapped a hoof and bleated. Why, he wondered, would there be a bone out on the moor unless ... unless ...

... it was one of the beast's victims!

Shaun watched as understanding dawned in Bitzer's eyes. The bone dropped from his mouth. Horrified, he spat and spluttered, wiping his tongue with both paws.

Shaun shook his head and crept into the gloom again. Bitzer traipsed after his friend and walked straight into him.

Shaun was as still as a statue, staring.

There was something in the darkness ahead: a long shape with two spiky looking claws, or were they teeth? A strange muttering drifted through the fog...

"Ere kitty itty itty... ereittyitty... itty..."

The beast! And it was calling for its mate.

Bitzer whimpered and glanced towards the safety of his doghouse. Shaun nudged him. This might be their only chance to surprise the beast. He was going to attack!

No! Bitzer's ears stood up in fright. Shaun would be snapped up in a single bite!

Too late.

Shaun launched himself at the strange shape, clinging on for dear life as the beast gave a bloodcurdling screech and tried to shake him off.

Bitzer heard a loud thump!, then Shaun bleating in shock.

And again: THUMP!

With one last glance over his shoulder at his doghouse, Bitzer screwed his courage. Shaun was in trouble. Bitzer bounded to the rescue ... only to skid to a halt.

Shaun hadn't found a beast at all. He had found an Old Lady with pink hair, sitting on a bench. Upset at being attacked by a sheep, she had Shaun over her knees and was thumping his tail with her handbag. Bitzer snickered, wincing as the bag landed on Shaun's bottom with another hefty whack.

"Errroffoutofit," the Old Lady mumbled, glaring as Shaun finally managed to struggle off her lap and totter away towards Bitzer.

Ten minutes later Bitzer was still giggling. Shaun muttered to himself, annoyed. Suddenly, he stopped walking.

Another dark figure loomed out of the fog. Shaun poked Bitzer. It was his turn to tackle the beast. Bitzer's giggles trailed off. Whatever the creature was, it was so big that its head was lost in the mist above. Shaun poked him again. What was he waiting for?

Bitzer squeezed his eyes closed, wondering what it would be like to be gobbled up. He crept nervously towards the dark shape. Perhaps if he was quiet whatever it was wouldn't notice him...

Snorting behind his hoof, Shaun patted him on the shoulder. Bitzer cried out and opened his eyes. He had caught a tree. A poster had been pinned to the trunk.

MISSING CAT

MR MITTENS
White and fluffy and smells of talcum powder.

If you see this puss call MOSSY BOTTOM 4225

REWARD:
Packet of biscuits (Missing)
3

Shaun shook his head, sadly. The beast had claimed another victim. This time a poor little kitty.

Shaun gulped. He nodded towards the barn. Perhaps they ought to think about making their way back?

OWWWW

Bitzer put his head on one side, as if he was thinking about it and then nodded slowly with a quiet whuff. Obviously, they both wanted to find the beast, but it was difficult to see anything in this terrible fog.

Then, trying not to look as though they were hurrying, the two of them started walking back towards the farm. Just a nice, quiet evening stroll...

OW-OW-OW-OW-ooooooooooo!

Bitzer tore past Shaun, running for his life.

A second after that, Shaun overtook Bitzer, bleating loudly as they passed the Old Lady again. The beast was coming! She had to save herself!

Tutting under her breath, she carried on with her knitting.

Chapter Five

OPERATION BEAST TRAP

The Flock had gathered. In the middle of the barn, several objects had been covered in a white sheet and an old wooden box was set before them. Shaun rapped the box with a stick.

None of the Flock took any notice. Hazel was too busy outlining a plan for catching the beast. The sheep should dig a deep hole, cover it with leaves and put a pizza in the middle...

Bleating loudly, the Twins suggested moving somewhere the beast would never find them, like a tropical island paradise. They were already wearing their snorkels and flippers.

Nuts' plan was even simpler. If the Flock made him some armour from old pots and pans and put a saddle on one of the pigs, he would ride into battle against the beast.

Shaun tapped the stick again and bleated loudly. The Flock needed to listen! As long as the beast was out there, no one was safe.

Finally, silence fell.

With a flourish, Shaun pulled away the sheet to reveal a diagram that spread across three blackboards.

Ta-dah!

The Flock held its breath. What was it? Some sort of funfair ride?

Shaun bleated. No – it was a trap. A trap from which the beast would never escape. A trap that would save the animals of Mossy Bottom Farm!

Tap, tap, tap, tap. The tip of Shaun's stick moved across the diagram. The beast would enter here, setting off this gizmo, which would move that widget and make the thingy whirl around, and so on and so forth.

The Flock gasped. All eyes were on Shaun. They would have to work hard, he bleated, marching up and down in front of them, hooves behind his back. There was a lot to do. The beast would be on the prowl again that very night, hunting for another victim. The trap would have to be built today.

Luckily, the Farmer would be out at Mossy Bottom Market.

Shaun looked around at the wide-eyed sheep. *Any questions?*

All the sheep shook their heads. Except Hazel. She raised a hoof, bleating nervously. Shaun's trap looked a teeny weeny bit on the complicated side. Couldn't they just dig a hole and cover it with leaves and put a pizza in it?

Shaun tapped a board again. This beast wouldn't be fooled by a hole in the ground covered with leaves, but it would be be fooled by a trap as complicated as this.

A familiar sound started in the distance. It was the rattle and clank of the tractor. The Farmer was leaving. It was time to get started!

Disappointed, the Twins took off their snorkels.

Confused chickens and puzzled pigs looked on as the Flock formed a chain of sheep. What were they up to now? The Flock was making a mechanical sheep robot with laser eyes to hunt the beast, clucked the chickens. The pigs squealed mockingly. The sheep were obviously creating a beast-detecting tank. Why else would they need a wind-up gramophone?

Shaun ignored them. He was bleating directions at the sheep like a sergeant major. One by one, bits of old junk passed along the chain: a mouldy slipper, a bicycle wheel, a gramophone, ropes and knotted string, an old scythe, a deflated football... On and on it went.

Dripping with sweat, sheep carried them out onto the moor, past the place where Shaun and Bitzer had found the bone – they gave the Old Lady on the bench a wide berth – until they came to the tree. After looking at the distant horizons of Soggy Moor, Shaun had decided it was the perfect place for a trap.

As the pile of rubbish grew, Bitzer ticked each item off his clipboard, occasionally poking one of the sheep and pointing back to the dump. The trap did not need a singing fish, a dead plant or a rat, no matter how happy the rat, called Barnaby, was to help.

A startled bleat made Shaun look up.

Before work could start again, Shirley had to be rescued from the runaway shopping trolley, Timmy untangled from his kite string, and Nuts pushed off the gramophone where he had been crying "Wheee" and going round and round and round until he was dizzy.

Eventually, however, the trap began to take shape. Sheep in welders' helmets and heavy gloves leaned over the shopping trolley, sparks flying. When they had finished, they lifted their masks, grinning and high-fiving. The first part of the trap was ready.

Bitzer put another tick on his clipboard, and moved onto where the Twins were glueing cracked mugs to a bicycle wheel. Another tick.

With spectacles perched on the ends of their noses, the Twins sucked pencils and watched a tennis ball roll down a length of rusty drainpipe. One shook his head. It was wrong, all wrong. After replacing the tennis ball with a turnip, they tried again. *Success!* Bitzer added yet another tick, and moved on. Behind him, sheep handed a rope to the chickens and told them to heave.

Meanwhile, Shaun rubbed out a set of complicated sums and started again. If a cup divided by a rubber duck equalled x, and a length of hairy string was y, then, taking into account the weight of a small fish, z must be an old wellington boot. A pig snatched the chalk out of his hand and corrected the board: x over y equalled a broken umbrella. Tutting, Shaun crossed out the pig's maths and added a spoon.

The pig gasped. Shaun punched the air. Not only would the trap work, but he had proved that the whole universe was held together with hairy string.

The chickens began clucking in panic. Bitzer ducked as the shopping trolley swung past at head height.

Whoosh!

He peered over Shaun's shoulder, nodded and ticked his clipboard. He didn't understand the maths, but it looked impressive. It was definitely worth a tick.

When the last string had been tied and the gramophone wound up, Shaun stood back to admire the Flock's handiwork. Chickens and pigs and even the ducks gave a round of applause. One chicken raised a wing, clucking. *It was really, really nice ... but what was it?*

Shaun grinned and bleated. It was a trap. And it was perfect!

All it needed was bait.

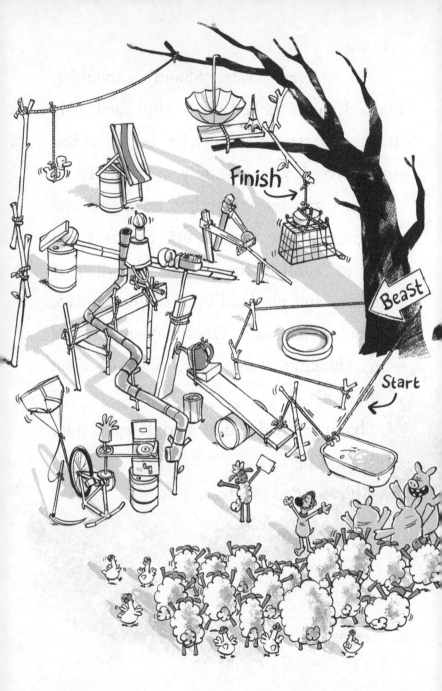

Chapter Six
TO CATCH A BEAST

Nuts stuck his arm in the air, hopping from one foot to the other in excitement and bleating loudly. He really, really wanted to be the bait.

Shaun ignored him, looking around the Flock for a sheep who looked tastier and less ... well ... peculiar. His gaze settled on Shirley. She was plump and juicy, just the sort of sheep to tempt a beast into the trap.

As if she could read Shaun's mind, Shirley scowled back fiercely. There was NO WAY she was going in the trap!

Behind her, Nuts jumped up and down.

Shaun's gaze moved on to young and tender Timmy. Before he could open his mouth, his vision was filled with the angry face of Timmy's Mum. *Don't even think about it*. With one hoof, she prodded Shaun in the chest. It was his trap, why didn't he sit in it and wait for the beast?

Shaun sighed. His eyes scanned back and forth across the Flock and finally rested on Nuts. All right, he agreed. Nuts could be the bait.

Nuts spun round the moor in joy. He was going to sit out in the cold all night, waiting for a ravenous monster to pounce on him. It was thrilling!

By now, the sun was slipping down towards the horizon. Soon the beast would be on the prowl, and the Farmer would be back from market.

With nervous glances towards the farmhouse, Bitzer flapped his paws and herded the sheep back to the barn while Shaun showed Nuts to his place. He must sit in the middle of an empty paddling pool that had been put in exactly the right spot...

Nuts' eyes crossed with the effort of thinking. He bleated slowly. What if the trap didn't work properly? What if he needed to escape?

Shaun gave him a pat on the back, and waved a hoof at the tangle of ropes and strings and kites and old drainpipes and rubber ducks and a shopping trolley. What could possibly go wrong?

* * *

"Baaa," said Nuts, nervously looking around. The beast was late.

Out on the moor, something moved.

Back in the barn, the Flock gathered around Shaun and Bitzer. Everyone was jittery. Bitzer was trying to look cool, which was difficult when he kept covering his eyes at the slightest noise. Hazel's teeth chattered, and Shirley was biting her hooves, although Shaun thought she might just be hungry. All they could do now was wait...

Outside, an owl hooted.

The Flock ran to the door. It opened with a creak, just enough for the Flock and Bitzer to peer out into the night. Shaun's eyes strained to see, but the trap was too far away. He could just about hear Nuts' anxious bleat.

YES! The turning bicycle wheel had wound the gramophone up. Shaun could hear the scratchy sound of a song called "You Are My Sunshine" in the distance. Any moment now the breeze would catch Timmy's kite...

"Whuff!" Bitzer pointed in excitement as he caught a glimpse of a silhouette. The Farmer's old underpants soared above the tree, dragging the old scythe behind them. It cut through a string that was holding—

Sheep high-fived when they heard the distant plop of a rubber duck, setting off a mechanism that involved a deckchair, a broken umbrella and a plastic model of the Eiffel Tower, which knocked out a peg that held the upside-down shopping trolley in place.

Cheers filled the barn as the trolley dropped down, trapping whatever was beneath it.

THE BEAST HAD BEEN CAUGHT!

Sheep hooked front legs, swinging each other in a jig. *No more beast!* At last, they were safe. Excited noises could be heard across the farm. Cockerels crowed, pigs squealed, ducks quacked, and the Farmer stuck his head out of a window, bellowing "Hurrupoorot!"

Shaun put a hoof to his lips, tipping his head and flapping his other hoof for quiet. He wanted to listen.

To what?

The Flock fell silent, leaning towards him. What could Shaun hear?

Shivering, Shaun stared into the night. That was the problem.

He couldn't hear anything: No growls of a beast trapped beneath an upside-down shopping trolley and – even worse – no Nuts.

Outside, the moor was strangely, eerily silent.

CHAPTER SEVEN

DAWN OF THE DREAD

A procession of anxious animals wound through the gap in the wall and across the moor. Chickens clucked and wiped tears from their beaks. Timmy's Mum dabbed at her eyes with a hankie. Bitzer pulled his hat off. Shaun felt a lump rising in his throat as he remembered Nuts' eager face. He should have listened to Timmy's Mum. *He* should've faced the beast, not Nuts.

Mist curled around the shopping trolley in the faint light of dawn. One of its wheels squeaked as it spun slowly in the breeze.

Shaun gulped. There was no sign of Nuts. By some freak accident, he must have been caught in the trap with the beast. Shaun tried not to think of the poor sheep's last moments – the flashing claws and fangs gleaming white in the moonlight as the beast—

With a yelp, Shaun almost jumped out of his wool. A face was pressed against the bars of the shopping trolley: an evil, hissing, spitting face. The beast was still in the trap – and so was Nuts!

They had to get Nuts out of there... Shaun blinked, surprised.

The beast was much, much smaller than he had expected, and Nuts wasn't screaming in terror. He was grinning and waving.

He was alive! And he had made a ... friend!

Nuts smothered the little beast in sloppy kisses. The beast scratched his face with sharp claws as it yowled and fought to get away.

Shaun gave Bitzer a questioning look. He couldn't help noticing that the beast wasn't particularly beastly. There was only one head. Its claws, while sharp, weren't as long as pickaxes.

In fact, the beast looked exactly like Mittens, the missing kitty. Shaun pointed to the poster that was nailed to the tree.

Bitzer shook his head, firmly. He had seen the actual shadow of the actual beast. He made a shape with his paws. It had been huge!

Hmm... Shaun crossed his arms and looked doubtful.

Hazel gave an urgent bleat: Look out!

The breeze had blown the last shreds of mist away and the rising sun cast the shadow of a huge creature across the ground. As one, the Flock gasped as it opened its cruel beak and ... chirped!

With a bleat, Shaun pointed to the tree. No, this wasn't the beast either, it was just a small robin, its shadow stretched out by the angle of the sun.

Shaun bleated thoughtfully. Had Bitzer really seen a beast with five heads? Or just the shadow of a cat stretched out by the moon?

Bitzer shuffled his feet and gave Shaun an ashamed grin. He might have exaggerated just a teeny weeny bit about the number of heads, but ... but—

Arrrooo-ooow! Ow-ow-ow-ooooooooo!

The Flock cowered. Bitzer held up a paw. *There!* The beast *was* real.

Shaun scratched his head. In bright daylight, the beast's wail sounded familiar. Exactly like a sound he'd heard just a few days ago when the Farmer had his wheelbarrow accident. Sure enough, the Farmer could be seen, through the kitchen window, hopping around and clutching his toe as if he had just stubbed it. Shaun thought about the Farmer's other recent mishaps...

Shaun blinked as he remembered the bandage around the Farmer's nose yesterday. The Farmer was clumsy. Might he have cut himself while trimming his nose hairs the night Bitzer had seen the beast's shadow? Had the second howl been the Farmer jumping into a bath without testing how hot the water was again?

Hmm. With another suspicious glance at Bitzer, Shaun plucked the clipboard out of his paws. He riffled through the pages. After finding the one he wanted, he counted the chickens. As he suspected! There were none missing. Bitzer had miscounted.

The bone they had found must have been one of Bitzer's, the wailing was just the clumsy Farmer, and the beast ... well, the beast was the shadow of a small but very nasty cat that needed to be returned to its owner.

Bitzer whuffed. He wrung his hat between his front paws and tried a smile. At least there would be a reward for taking the cat back: a packet of biscuits (three missing) that he would be happy to share.

CHAPTER EIGHT
THE MEADOW OF FEAR

Night had fallen, and mist was creeping across Mossy Bottom Farm once more. Singing "Pump um pum de pum" under his breath, Bitzer checked his clipboard.

At his side, Shaun yawned. It was nearly bedtime. It had been a long day, but a good one. They had solved the mystery of the Beast of Soggy Moor and reunited the Old Lady and her cat.

In the barn, Shirley was putting cucumber over her eyes while Timmy's Mum told Timmy bedtime stories of the terrifying beast. The Farmer was safely in the farmhouse with a new bandage around his toe. The ducks were playing cards, and the pigs were snoring like bulldozers. Shaun smiled. Tomorrow night, he decided, he would put a sheet over his head and jump out on Bitzer—

Grrrrrrrrrrroooooowwwwlllll!

Bitzer and Shaun stopped. Turning to face each other, they grinned. What had the Farmer done this time? Bitzer put one final tick on his clipboard and whuffed good night to Shaun. Shaun trotted off to the barn and bed.

As he disappeared inside, a gust of wind blew across the farmyard, slapping a piece of paper to the wall...

ACTIVITIES

HOW TO CATCH
A BEAST

Can you draw the perfect trap? What will you use to make it? What kind of beast will you catch?

MATERIALS
A pencil
A large piece of paper
Your imagination

HOW TO DRAW BITZER

MATERIALS

Pencils
A large sheet of paper

STEP 1 Copy the shape
in the diagram. (It looks
a bit like a nose!)

STEP 2 Give your
"nose" two legs.

STEP 3 Add droopy
balloon shapes. (These
are Bitzer's ears.)

STEP 4 Draw Bitzer's mouth. This is a curved line that loops back on itself at one end.

STEP 5 Add a circle for Bitzer's nose. Then draw his hat, which is a half circle with a curved line for the rolled brim. Copy the picture here.

STEP 6 Give Bitzer some teeth and eyes. You can add colour too if you want.

MAKE A
PAPER TELEPHONE

It's perfect for keeping in touch while on a beast hunt.

<u>MATERIALS</u>

2 paper cups
A sharp pencil
String (8 metres long)
A pair of scissors
A friend

STEP 1 Poke a small hole in the bottom of each cup using the sharp pencil. (Ask a parent or guardian to help you.)

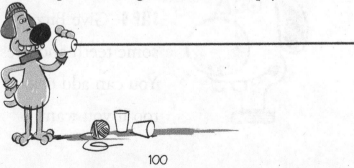

STEP 2 Thread the string through the hole in one of the cups. Tie a knot to secure it. Repeat with the other cup.

STEP 3 You and your friend each take one cup and then move away from each other until the string is pulled taut.

STEP 4 One person talks into the cup and the other holds the cup to his or her ear. What can you hear? Is the beast nearby?

Tales from Mossy Bottom Farm

FLOCK TO THE SEASIDE

An excerpt from
the new book in the series!

Chapter One
BIG DAY OUT

In the trailer behind the Farmer's car, Shaun and the Flock bounced along green and leafy country lanes on a hot summer's day. As swallows dipped and swooped around them, sheep bleated and hung their heads over the sides of the trailer, enjoying the breeze and the sights of the open road.

Shaun's favourite sight was the Farmer's bald head banging against the roof of the car to shouts of "Bah!" and "Ooo-aaaargh!" every time they hit a bump in the road.

Bitzer was next to him. His head was stuck out of the window, one paw on his hat to stop it blowing away, and his tongue was fluttering in the wind like a pink flag.

Shaun held on tight as the wheels hit an especially big bump. The Flock bleated to one another. With every mile, their curiosity grew. Where was the Farmer taking them on such a beautiful day?

Timmy was dreaming of the seaside. Shirley hoped they were going out to lunch at a restaurant with a dessert trolley so large that it took three waiters to push it. The Twins wanted to go to a rock festival to see their favourite band, **THE REVOLVING CUCUMBERS.**

Nuts was sure they were going to a show. He'd even brought some chocolate-covered raisins he'd found sprinkled over the floor of the rabbit hutches to share out during the interval. He peered into the paper bag. The rabbits were mad to leave perfectly good chocolate-covered raisins lying about like that.

His thoughts were interrupted by an excited bleat from Shaun, who was leaning over the side of the trailer and pointing a hoof. Through a gap in the trees, Nuts caught a glimpse of something that was deep blue, sparkling and dotted with white. The Farmer wasn't taking them to the theatre.

He was taking them to the seaside!

The Flock bleated delightedly as the car clanked over the top of a hill. The sea spread out before them, stretching to the horizon. Even better, in the distance were the stripy tents, helter-skelters and rollercoasters of a funfair. The breeze smelled of candyfloss and suntan cream.

Squeezing his eyes closed in concentration, Timmy reached into Shirley's fleece and pulled out a bucket and spade. Reaching in again, he found a pair of armbands and a surfboard. Happy sheep beamed at each other. Grinning, Shaun started three bleats for the Farmer: "Bleat, bleat-ooo-ooooo..."

The second bleat turned into a wail as the car turned sharply. The Flock were thrown from one side of the trailer to the other and almost tipped out. Then, on two wheels instead of four, the car screeched through an open gate and skidded to a halt in a field.

"Bleat," finished Shaun in quiet disgust.

The meadow was filled with familiar sights. Farmers in muddy green coats and wellington boots stood sipping tea and eating sandwiches outside a small tent. Through the open flap of another tent, Shaun could see men poking an enormous marrow and making notes.

There were stalls selling **LARRY STILES' SHEEP DIP** and **HOOF-U-LIKE OINTMENT** and **DOCTOR ULCER'S PIGGIN' LOVELY PIG RUB**. A sign that read **"THE GREAT-PIDDLINGTON-ON-SEA ANNUAL FARM EXTRAVAGANZA"** hung from the front of a trestle table, behind which sat three judges with rosettes pinned to their jackets.

In the centre of it all was a large green space dotted with hurdles and pens.

The Flock peered over the side of the trailer and groaned. They weren't going to the seaside after all. The Farmer had brought them to a farm show, and that could only mean one thing: a sheepdog trial!

There wasn't even an ice-cream van.

Meanwhile, the Farmer had spotted

the tea tent. "Oooyumnumnum," he cried, rubbing his hands together. Glancing towards Bitzer, he jerked his thumb over his shoulder towards the Flock and barked an order before striding away, licking his lips.

Bitzer jumped out of the car, clipboard in paw. He stared at the largest of the gold cups on the judges' table with stars in his eyes. He had heard about this trial. It was legendary among sheepdogs. Only the best – the *very* best – could hope to win the **GREAT-PIDDLINGTON-ON-SEA ANNUAL FARM EXTRAVAGANZA GOLD CUP FOR BEST SHEEPDOG**. A look of determination crossed his face. This time he wouldn't accidentally herd the Flock into the toilet tent. The cup would be his.

But first, he had to prepare. After unhooking the back of the trailer, he peeped his whistle to order the sheep out into the field. He tapped the clipboard with his pencil as they shoved and jostled around him. In a moment he would direct them to a holding pen to wait their turn, but first he needed to take them through a few tactics and moves.

Shaun held up a hoof, bleating and sniggering. Would these be like the tactics Bitzer used at the last trial, where he had tried to impress the judges by wearing rollerskates and had herded the sheep straight into a toilet?

Bitzer scowled, remembering how he had skated through a cowpat and accidentally splattered it all over the judges. Ignoring Shaun, he showed the sheep the clipboard. At the start of the course, they would form Bitzer Herding Formation A and proceed in an orderly fashion to—

Scornful laughter interrupted him.

Bitzer turned round. Behind him a dog in a "**TOP DOG**" baseball cap leaned against a holding pen that contained perfectly straight lines of sheep. Each of them had an electronic device clipped to one ear. In one paw, the dog held a gadget that looked like a mobile phone. He also had an expensive-looking earpiece and microphone. His eyes were hidden by mirror sunglasses. Chuckling, he shook his head at Bitzer's clipboard and tapped the screen of his device.

Bitzer's jaw dropped as a fizzle of electricity went through Top Dog's sheep. With a startled bleat, they all jumped into a perfect circle.

Top Dog tapped his screen again. Another fizz of electricity buzzed through his flock and they all leaped back into lines.

With a sneering whuff, he flashed his phone at Bitzer. Clipboards and whistles were *soooo* old-fashioned. *Everyone* had an eHerder these days. It made herding simple, plus it could be used as a telephone and to take photos...

Bitzer, too, looked like he'd been electrocuted. Seconds passed as he stared, mouth hanging open, at the eHerder, until Top Dog snickered again and pointed over Bitzer's shoulder.

Bitzer tore his gaze from the gadget and glanced back at the Flock. They were ...

With a gulp, he turned slowly and blinked.

... they were *gone*.